STEPHANIE FLYNN

Small Fish Publishing
USA

This is a work of fiction. Names, characters, places, and incidents either are the products of the author's imagination or are used fictitiously. Any resemblance to actual persons, living or dead, businesses, companies, events, or locales is entirely coincidental.

Copyright © 2022 Stephanie Flynn

All rights reserved. This book or parts thereof may not be reproduced in any form, stored in any retrieval system, or transmitted in any form by any means—electronic, mechanical, photocopy, recording, or otherwise—without prior written permission of the author, except as provided by United States of America copyright law. For permission requests, write to the author Stephanie Flynn, subject line "Attention: Permission Request," at the address below.

stephanie@stephanieflynn.net

First edition

Cover design by Stephanie Flynn

ISBN eBook: 978-1-952372-70-4

ISBN paperback: 978-1-952372-71-1

To my inspiring crazy cats and all your weirdness, this is for you.
(Why won't you talk to me?!?)
(No, I'm not a crazy cat lady, I swear!)

Chapter 1

Followed

I squeezed an orange for fitness and added it to a thin plastic bag. It should've been an ordinary grocery run, but I couldn't shake this feeling of being watched. As I tied the bag, I scanned the big-box grocery store. A sprinkling of customers around me minded their own business. Not one of them looked at me. My patented grumpy face kept most everyone at bay, so of course, no one was watching me. I set the oranges in the basket at the crook of my arm.

My paranoia nagged just like my mother, Gracie, and her silly ideas for my life. Well, my life consisted of making dinner, washing dishes, and scrubbing floors. Sounded normal until I got to the part of showering my mother, washing her bedding, managing her medications and appointments. The grocery store was my temporary escape, and now my moment of peace was being ruined.

I glanced inconspicuously over my shoulder. And...no one suspicious. It had to be all in my head. I moved to another aisle and chose a box of noodles for tonight. Gracie always had her input, and I listened to her, but since she couldn't take care of herself any longer, the menu was my choice. I took a few steps and grabbed a jar of traditional red sauce to go with it. Oh, Gracie was going to give me words about it, but unless she wanted to blend up tomatoes and chop fresh herbs by herself—not happening—I was going to doctor this jar and she was going to like it.

With her extensive and exhausting care, perhaps something as basic as dinner was my one attempt to control an aspect of my life. I wasn't complaining. Life, lemons, lemonade and all that. But if I'd been born a witch like my mother, scrubbing the floors would've been so much easier.

With my extra perceptive senses, the feeling of being watched returned. I spun, and a man wearing dark jeans, a white T-shirt, and a blue unbuttoned shirt hanging loose like a jacket, stood near me. He was reading the label on a jar of sauce—the fancy Alfredo kind. Was he going to add shrimp to his fettuccine? That sounded amazing, but sadly, Gracie couldn't have dairy. As I stared, puzzled about why my brain was so bored I invented dinner plans for a stranger, he faced me.

I gasped like I was caught red-handed trying to steal his wallet.

He smiled, showing a bright gleam of white teeth and a crinkling at the corners of his gorgeous blue eyes. Thick, wavy dark hair with a few glistens of gray had me guessing late thirties, early forties. He was distinguished, handsome as hell, and someone I'd never seen in our small town before. Since Gracie set me up so many times, I thought I'd met everyone.

"Spaghetti, huh?" he asked, looking at my choices.

I tucked a stray lock of blond hair behind my ear. "Shrimp fettuccine Alfredo?"

The handsome stranger chuckled and returned the jar to the shelf. My eye caught on a talisman hanging around his neck—round, antique bronze, with a symbol carved into it. I'd never seen anything like it, but it looked old. "Just browsing. You know, killing time."

Killing time in a grocery store but not shopping. This sexy stranger sure was intriguing. "Why here? There's a bar down the block and a park in the opposite direction."

"I'm not a drinker, and I don't have a use for parks. I'm here for a little business, and a little for personal reasons." The stranger swept his piercing blue eyes over me from my messy bun to skinny jeans and ankle booties.

Heat tore through my body.

Chapter 2

Hope Sinks

I SHIFTED THE WEIGHT of the shopping basket in my arm and stepped closer to the sexy stranger, wanting to catch a whiff of his scent.

"Well, when I have free time…which… Huh," I sputtered, attempting to share an idea for alleviating boredom, but I'd never had that problem. Gracie kept me on my toes all the time, except when she pushed me into blind dates. I always argued against it, but ultimately, I surrendered for the sake of her stubbornness and bedtime routine. My patented grumpy face meant most dates were a bust. Like this stranger, I had no use for bars or the parks, and apparently no better ideas to offer.

"You're never bored," he finished for me. "You must lead an exciting life. Those exotic oranges just reek of a well-traveled tongue."

Heat rushed up my throat and cheeks. Speaking of well-traveled... "I thought I knew everyone in town, but I've never seen you before. Are you new here or just passing through?" *Please say new, please say new.*

"I've been around. Actually, I have a place nearby, but I'm not there much. Work keeps me busy." He glanced away, tipping his face up over the shelf as if looking for someone.

Now he made sense. Of course, a sexy man wouldn't be 'killing time' alone in a grocery store. He had someone here he was waiting for, and now I hoped an angry or jealous woman wouldn't come claw my eyes out. I couldn't afford any more humiliation in this small town. With the stories floating around of me being cold, heartless, and generally grumpy around men, I was surprised he was willing to talk to me at all. Then again, he seemed different from the men Gracie had scrounged together. But just as quick as it began, it was over. "Oh, I didn't mean to get in your way. Don't let me hold you back from whoever—"

The stranger focused on me again. "You're not. I'm Mikeal, by the way." He struck out a hand.

I shook it, a quiver of nerves dancing all along my body. "Maggie. Nice to meet you."

"Pleasure is all mine." He leaned forward as if he were going to kiss my knuckles, but he didn't. He released me and stood up straight, but his eyes swept along my body again. "There's not much going on in this town. What do you do for a living?"

The first man I had any interest in whatsoever was now going to run for the hills. Like I said, just as quick as it began, it was over. Too bad because Gracie would've liked him. "I'm my mother's full-time caretaker. She's sick."

"I'm sorry to hear that in more ways than one."

I tilted my head, confused about his sympathy, but I didn't want to be rude. "Thank you. What kind of work in this dreadfully small town could possibly keep you so busy I've never seen you before?"

Mikeal's piercing blue eyes met mine. "A job I wish I could quit."

"Then do it." That sounded like an easy answer to a simple problem, unlike mine.

Mikeal smiled. "If only it were that easy. Speaking of which, I truly must be going. It's been a pleasure to finally meet you, Maggie. Maybe I'll see you around."

Finally? He was still interested despite my reputation. I smiled like a loony. "I'd like that."

Before I could ask for his digits, he disappeared around the corner. And he didn't offer them to me either. So much for interested. Knowing my luck and severe lack of free time, I needed to stomp that hope until it was dead. It was a useless mindset.

Chapter 3

The Plea

AFTER DINNER, I SCRUBBED the dishes, but my brain had been stuck on Mikeal with the piercing blue eyes. Gracie always insisted I find someone to marry. In her feeble condition, no matter how much she protested, she needed my help. Until she moved beyond the veil, I'd happily bring her soup and wash the floors, since her magic was weakening along with her body. Our remaining time was short, and I had plenty of years left to figure myself out afterward, but I didn't want to think about that. I never wanted to choose to place some stranger ahead of my mother's needs. And that meant Mikeal was just a fantasy who lived on in my memory.

Besides, he didn't leave me his phone number. I sighed and moved the wash rag in mindless circles.

"Margaret Mae Jones, what did you do this time?" Gracie asked with stern disappointment on her tongue. "I heard it didn't go well."

Oh, the use of my full name meant I was in trouble. I rinsed the plate and settled it on the drying rack. We'd had this same conversation so many times I considered joining a convent to escape it, but as none would ever accept what I was, it was just an idle thought. "He wouldn't stop staring at his phone, so I gave him something to stare at."

Arms crossed over her soft chest, Gracie waited for details of my last blind date from hell—Kyle. His name alone made me shiver.

I rolled my eyes and reached for another plate. "An empty chair, okay? I ditched Kyle at the restaurant. He went on and on about...fantasy football, I think? I don't know. His face was glued to his phone and clearly, he wasn't interested. I'm not sure how long it took him to notice my absence, but he deserved to be stiffed with the check."

"Again? Is this the face you greeted him with? Are you deliberately sabotaging your happiness?" Gracie grumbled. Before I could get a word of defense in, she asked, "Did you hear what happened to poor Lucy at the grocery store?"

I was there earlier and heard nothing, but a flash of Fantasy Mikeal's smiling face sent a bloom of heat through my chest. "No, what?"

Using her hands, Gracie mimicked a building tipping over and crashing to the ground. "Dead, just like that. She was alone for years, poor miserable thing, and I don't want that for you. Perhaps Kyle wasn't the one, but there's someone out there for you."

I dipped the next plate into the soapy water. "I'm not miserable, and I'm not alone. Newsflash, I'm washing *our* dishes, and you're right beside me, unless I'm seeing ghosts. You're not a ghost, right?" I jested.

"Maggie, my dear, I'm not going to be around forever."

I dried my hands on a towel and turned to face my mom. I gripped her hands in mine. "I was kidding. I'm happy to be here for you for however long I still have you. Now stop with the doom-and-gloom, okay?"

Her deep brown eyes sparkled with worry. "One day you're going to be old like me, and I don't want you to wallow in loneliness. You need to settle down before it's too late."

I hugged my mom. We were two peas from very different pods. "I've been taking care of you all these years. That proves I'm capable of taking care of myself. Don't worry about me. I promise I'm happy, and I will be happy no matter what happens." The words rang hollow, but I smiled through them.

Chapter 4

Bad Idea

My mother Gracie pulled back from my hug and flinched at the ache in her leg. I checked the time. She wasn't due for her next pain reliever for another half hour, but Gracie didn't complain. She was admirably strong, always had been, but stubborn as a mule too. And the older she got, the more she pestered me. We'd had this conversation so many times, but it never went anywhere but me agreeing to another blind date. At this point, I don't think anyone could be considered 'blind' anymore. There couldn't possibly be any single men left in this town that I hadn't gone on a date with. And I was done with all that, no matter her attempts at reasoning or begging.

"I don't believe you, and since I won't be able to say, '*I told you so*' from beyond the grave, I'm going to set you up right."

I swallowed back an actual growl. Not again. "Please, don't. Really, I don't want any more blind dates, and would you quit talking about the grave? I love you, Mom. It stresses me out when you talk about dying all the time. You're fine." That was a lie. The endless medications attested to it, but the stress and the love parts were true.

"Fine. I have a plan that will solve all your troubles, and I promise no more talking about the grave, okay?"

I cast her my patented side-eye and said, suspiciously, "Sure."

Gracie beamed, and with a wave of her fingers and a mumble of words, she cast a spell. Swirls of glowing magic spun over her open palm. A stack of papers appeared out of thin air. Gracie had claimed she couldn't animate the mop to do her floor washing. I wasn't sure if I believed that, but since she didn't find satisfaction watching me labor away, I gave her the benefit of the doubt. Unfortunately, I wasn't born with the gene to practice magic, or I would've animated the mop myself. No, I got something else entirely—like I'd explained, two very different pods.

Gracie's excited smile lit up as she silently read the top page.

"What's that?" I asked, dreading the answer.

"Maggie, you've rejected every man I've brought to you, and I think I found the pattern."

Great, psychoanalyzed by an elderly and biased woman. "You're lucky you're old and cute."

Gracie beamed. She meant well, but she never took a hint, even when it was bright, glowing, and beeping incessantly. "You need someone different than the cutie patooties I find at the store. You need a man who's clever, quick, and playful, just like you, and I know just how to do it."

Gracie was crafty, and not in the needlepoint way. A lump formed high in my throat. By now, I was sure I'd rejected all of the eligible men in this town. "What are you up to now?"

"You'll see." With a flick of her wrist, the papers soared out the window like an old printing press, ready to be fixed to light posts, left on benches, and stuck to shop windows all over town.

I groaned. That couldn't be anything good. I didn't know how else to discourage whatever nauseating matchmaking she planned this time. "These days we use the internet, Mom, so good luck with your papers. By the way, good job keeping your magic on the down-low. I'm going to bed."

Gracie smiled deviously, and I went to my room, already dreading the next man I had to shoo away.

Unless it was Mikeal.

Nah, he was a fantasy. I shooed him away too.

Chapter 5

Rules

Thunderous pounding on the door wrenched me from my fitful sleep. Pressing a hand against my throbbing forehead, I climbed out of bed and shuffled to the door, wishing for coffee before having to do adult things. I gazed through the peephole and blinked twice, trying to process what stood on our doorstep—a half a dozen men—differing in age, clothing, and attractiveness. Kyle was in the group, whom I'd previously ditched. I couldn't figure out what these men had in common.

While I watched, they conversed with each other. Some roughhoused a little. A pair puffed their peacock feathers at each other in a show of dominance, reminding me of a family gathering, except these people weren't related.

"Mom, get out here," I called across our small house.

Gracie limped over to the door and groaned softly. I steadied her on her tiptoes, and she peeked through. A grin spread her lips. "Oh, they're here already."

"They? Who's they? What did you do, Mom? What was on those papers?"

Gracie patted my arm, a youthful glint in her eye. "A game to win your heart."

Here we go again. "I don't want any games. I don't want any matchmaking or blind dates. And Kyle is out there."

"This is precisely what you need. Trust me."

I snorted. "Actually, what I need is coffee and breakfast. So here's what's going to happen. I'm going to make us coffee while you tell all those guys out there to go home because whatever crazy game you advertised is off. After this mess goes away, I'll go pick up some breakfast." I shuffled to the kitchen and opened the upper cabinet door. Coffee aroma filled my nose, perking me up just a little. I grabbed the jug of coffee grounds.

Gracie followed and rested on a chair nearest to me. "I've been waiting for you to choose someone, but, my dear, I'm out of time."

I scooped grounds and dumped them into the filter. "I didn't see you shoo them away yet."

"And I'm not going to. The game states whichever man is the cleverest, quickest, and most playful will catch the key. I used those words specifically to keep the spirit of the game friendly and respectful, for safety."

"Key? What key?" I humored her while filling the glass carafe.

"This one." Gracie held out a copy of the front door key.

"You're going to toss it into the yard and let them fight for it? Seems a little crude." But it also sounded half entertaining...after I got my mitts around some wakey-wakey juice. My head still pounded.

"The man who wins the game is the one you will marry."

I scoffed at the ridiculousness. "And they're aware of that stipulation?" I couldn't believe Kyle showed up. He didn't give two craps about me on our date. What guy in this day and age would blindly marry someone after winning a game? This wasn't medieval times. This was Menominee, Michigan, a small town, mostly modern...and peaceful.

"Of course, they know. Believe it or not, Maggie, the men in this town find you fascinating. It wasn't hard to convince them to show up."

I turned on the pot. "I suppose I could watch them fight it out." And when the winner approached—not Kyle—I'd tell him, '*Thanks for the entertainment. Here's five bucks for your effort. Go home.*'

"You misunderstand. You'll have the key."

Gracie was hiding something, or she was being considerate, walking me through this plan of hers gently. I folded my arms across my chest and leaned against the counter.

Chapter 6

A Deal

I DIDN'T LIKE THIS key-game plan of hers, but it was different than any other matchmaking attempt so far. Kudos for creativity, but I wasn't going to take the rigid rules of her game at face value. I could be creative too. "Since I don't want a pack of desperate men to assault me, I guess that means I have to hide the key from them."

Gracie smiled. "At my age, you'd love a pack of hungry men waiting to jump your bones."

"First—that's gross, Mom. Second, at your age, they'd break all your bones."

Gracie laughed. "Oh, but it would be worth it. No better way to go out than with a bang."

The banter drained out of me. "We talked about this. No more end-of-days talk, okay?"

"Fine, fine. As long as you keep in spirit of the game, the plan is for you to hide the key."

Finally something reasonable. I could handle that. I dug in my pocket to see if I had five bucks to spare. I slipped a bill free. "When this is over, you promise no more of these antics?"

"I absolutely promise."

One last ruse and I was free. "Alright. Game on." Now, where was I going to stash that key so they wouldn't get it? Inside the house seemed pointless, and I didn't want to listen to their endless pounding on the door. It had to be outside. I smiled to myself. I could sit back, sip my warm coffee, and watch grown ass men scour the yard looking for the golden ticket like children hunting Easter eggs. I needed to get a pack of those bright plastic eggs to hide the key inside. Perhaps, after their frustration, twenty bucks would be a better offer.

"Perfect," Gracie said. With a swirl of her hand, magic rushed from her palm and circled me. My hair kicked up in a contained breeze, and a pressure formed around my body. I recognized this feeling, and I didn't like it one bit.

"Mom, what are you doing? You never said anything about forcing me to shift!"

Unlike my witch mother, I was a shifter, specifically a gray and black tabby cat. As I'd said, two very different pods. Thanks, Dad. Rest in peace. Instead of me pulling from the inside to shift into a small house cat, this pressure from the outside, courtesy of Gracie, was forcing me. Against my will, I shifted into my cat form, and Gracie grew as I shrunk. I never voluntarily spent time in this furry form. Too many people preferred their rifles rather than opening their doors to their cozy fireplaces. I would've rather had magic—then I wouldn't be in this mess.

I pawed my way out of my pile of clothes.

A satisfied smile danced on my mother's lips. She rummaged in her robe pocket and leaned down. I half expected her to pet me, which I also hated. Instead, she fastened a collar around my neck with something loose dangling from it. "You have the key to the front door. Until a man catches it, you're staying a cat."

"Mom, this is humiliating. Please don't."

Gracie pet me on the head, and I grimaced. She picked me up. "One day, you'll thank me."

Fat chance.

Gracie opened the door with me tucked in her arms like a football and announced to the impatient suitors, "On this cat's neck is the key. You read the rules. Whoever catches the cat gets the key to the front door and my daughter's hand in marriage. Play nice."

Some of the men chuckled with excitement. Others rubbed their hands together.

Gracie whispered, "The marriage is magically binding, so choose wisely."

Good thing divorce court wasn't.

I gave my mother the best attempt at a snarl I could, and she released me.

Chapter 7

Games Begin

From oral legends and written stories handed down throughout history, every member of the supernatural community knew to keep their mouths shut about the hidden world, and those who didn't faced consequences from others of their kind. Too many witches and shifters had been persecuted in fear over the centuries. Too many vampires, direct threats to normal humans, were slaughtered for simply existing. Now we were the minority. Even though I wanted to give a healthy slice of my mind to these men chasing me, I wouldn't risk it.

I tore off through alleys and nearby neighborhoods, anywhere just to escape and regroup. Some of the men climbed into a lifted pickup truck, leaving only a few men's footsteps pounding the pavement after me. But what human could catch a cat in a foot race? One willing to play this stupid game in the first place, and that meant not one of these 'suitors' was suitable at all. What had Gracie been thinking?

I leaped onto a brick wall. My fur was disheveled and messy. I'd already been ornery before this charade started, but now I was hungry, thirsty—I hadn't gotten my morning coffee yet—and no one was watching over Gracie. Why would she do this to herself?

Well, as her level-headed caretaker, I was going to end it. I reached within myself and pulled, drawing my human form back out, but I was blocked. Gracie's magic wouldn't allow me to break the rules of her game.

I sighed in frustration. She really meant to have me marry one of these men. How was I supposed to make a reasonable choice when my entire livelihood depended on it? This was more like a case of 'the best of the bad options considering the circumstances'. How were these constraints supposed to lead to any kind of long-term happiness? Considering the wild chase and the improbability of these men giving me a two-minute break, I focused internally and estimated the next hairball due time.

A rustle caught my sensitive ears.

"Gotcha!" one man said sharply as his hands darted for me.

I leaped away and wanted to snark at him about giving advanced warning when attempting to be stealthy, but like the rules of our world, my shifter status was firmly in the hush-hush category. I'd never open up to anyone about it, and I'd never met another shifter to share with. Not even my own mother understood. At least with magic, she looked human all the time, and frankly, having magic seemed so convenient.

I bolted off through a line of bushes and over a white privacy fence, focusing on the estimated hairball time again, determining I should've been free from the involuntary convulsing for at least a day or two. That was one minor relief. Yep, magic would've been a far better alternative.

Cats were fast, but they specialized in sprinting, not marathons. Out of sight, perhaps I could rest here. I sashayed through the backyard, on the lookout for a residual puddle or dog dish or any water, but no luck. Parched and tired, I curled up under a shrub and waited until the initial excitement of the game passed. Then I could go home and talk sense into my mother, or paw at her lap incessantly until she gave in and released me from this...curse.

Pricking up my ears, people nearby tended to whatever they were doing—setting up the grill, hammering something in their garage, watering flowers. Nothing caught my attention as suspicious, so when a net flung down over the shrub to the grass around me, I was genuinely surprised.

"Oh, I got you." The voice made me shrink with disgust: fantasy football Kyle, a sandy haired, medium build, average guy. His appearance wasn't an issue; it was his personality, reminding me of a piece of gum stuck to the bottom of my favorite shoes—clingy, noisy, embarrassing. His gloat came out as a sharp cackle. "I'm the winner. I knew it! None of those other guys are smart enough to catch a cat.

Unfortunately for me, it's against the law to shoot wild game in the city limits, but since I'm an excellent hunter, the net had to suffice." He tugged on the net, trying to scoop me into it with the shrub in the way.

"Now don't you move. I just need to get you free of this bush and that crazy old bat can have you back." He looked at me thoughtfully. "What? I need to stay on her good side until she kicks off." Kyle fought, trying to grab me while using the net as a barrier, but the shrub interfered.

If that was what he thought of Gracie, what did he think of me? I didn't care enough to stick around. I found a gap between the metal frame of the round net and the grass beneath my feet. I wriggled free and darted away, dodging the metaphorical, and almost literal, bullet.

"Damn it! Get back here, you stupid cat!"

Ah yes, I was the stupid one. I trotted through backyards and leaped over more fences, tongue going drier by the second. If Gracie intended for me to outsmart all but one of these men, thus dragging out the game, why couldn't she have let me eat and have coffee first? I bet she wanted me to be miserable, so I'd end this game as quick as possible. Well, I wasn't picking the love of my life in two seconds.

The sounds of men plotting their hunt pricked my ears. "It went that way." Kyle's voice. "Ty, you head this way, and I'll take that way."

Based on the rules of the game, I couldn't imagine why two men would work together. Regardless of their puzzling motivation, I wasn't going to be shared. In the face of a brick wall, I leaped.

"There it is!" one man shouted to Kyle.

I trotted along the top of the brick wall around the perimeter and leaped back down to the grass on the other side. This was going to be exhausting if these guys didn't give up soon. But I'd rather stay a cat forever than marry any one of them.

Even if that meant nine lives of torture.

Chapter 8

Found

THE SUNLIGHT WAS WARM, but the air was dry and chilly with autumn. I slipped under a child's slide, shrouded safely in tall grasses the homeowner failed to weed whack. I licked at the shaded grass, trying to capture drops of remaining dew, but since it hadn't rained in days and morning was hours ago, I got nothing. My tongue stuck in my mouth like cotton. Running all the way to the river or the bay would take more energy than I had left. All I could do was go home with my tail between my legs, after the initial excitement ended.

However long that would take.

I sighed and curled into a ball, ready for a long cat nap. My eyelids closed and for a short while, I was left in peace.

"Hello, there," a masculine voice said, startling me out of my fur. In my cat form, sneaking up on me so easily was nearly impossible. I blinked my sleep away, and a pair of legs stood nearby. "You must be thirsty. Here."

Before I could dart away, a small familiar saucer was pushed near me. Water sloshed in the shallow dish. Still under the safety of the slide, I checked all angles for a net, but there weren't any. I checked for traps and even the barrel of a gun. Nothing. My parched throat urged me closer to the water, and I lapped it up, relishing in the heavenly feeling of a thirst finally quenched. I wanted to thank the man, but I couldn't risk it.

With the saucer emptied and my strength rejuvenated, I slipped out from under the slide, ready to bolt. A tall man—okay, everyone was tall in my cat form—bent over and collected the plate. As my eyes skimmed his clothes and the fascinating talisman around his neck, his dark hair slicked back with gel, and the trimmed beard on his angular jaw, my heart skipped a beat. Recognition dawned on me. *Mikeal?*

Mikeal stood up and sent me a friendly smile. "I hope this ends the way you wanted." He walked away with the plate.

I tilted my head. I didn't see him in the testosterone-fueled scuffle on my porch, but he had to know about the game, so why was he leaving? Intrigued, I jogged after him through the backyard and out to the street, but he was gone. I spun, seeking the handsome stranger, but somehow, he completely vanished. I had my tricks, but that was a new one to me.

"There it is," Kyle said, causing my blood to run extra cold. I shivered.

Across the street, congregating around a lifted pickup truck, Kyle and two other players homed in on me like robots targeting their prey. My breath caught in my throat.

"Go!" Kyle shouted, and at his orders, the three of them broke into a jog with the sandy haired fantasy football enthusiast leading the way. The menace on his face and the two others flanking him in the fading light was nightmarish. Kyle still carried his round metal net. One stranger wore leather work gloves, but the other was empty handed. At least none of them carried a gun.

At the closest porch, a wooden deck with a decorative lattice wrap-around, I found a gap and squeezed through. The men circled me like predators hungry for a meal. Hunting a cat had brought out their feral side. Normally I'd be relieved knowing they wouldn't actually eat me, but under these circumstances, I feared for worse. Regardless, like hell I was going to marry one of these monsters.

"Here, kitty, kitty. Come out, come out, wherever you are," Kyle sang a cliché tune.

Chapter 9

Hunted

I PRESSED MYSELF AGAINST the concrete foundation under the deck, unable to escape.

"Yeah, cat. Just give us the key, and you can be on your way," the gloved guy said.

I never exposed my shifter side to the public, and certainly not to Kyle. Funny how they thought a cat understood English. I shrugged.

"Hey, you," the empty-handed man whispered from the lattice nearest to me. Without weapons or self-defense equipment, he appeared the most trustworthy. "If you come close, I'll take that heavy key off your neck, and I promise I'll let you escape without anyone else hurting you." His fingers beckoned me closer.

The urge to say something, anything, and watch these men screech and scramble away was overwhelming.

Kyle laughed. "Aiden, cats don't understand you, and are you really planning on breaking our deal?"

Aiden turned away from me. "The deal's on, but being a jerk isn't going to get you want you want. Try some honey once in a while."

"If you have catnip on you, we can talk, but otherwise, less yakking and more plucking. I'll pay you both when we get the cat in the net," Kyle said.

By reason of deduction, the remaining guy wearing the leather gloves was Ty. He shifted his weight uncomfortably. "I don't know if this is worth the effort, Kyle. This is humiliating."

Likewise, my enemy, likewise.

"I went on a date with her," Kyle said. "Boring as hell, stubborn and cold, and a little weird. She's all about her crazy mother who claims to know magic."

I would've slapped my forehead if I could. *Gracie,* I silently scolded, *you know the rules!*

Ty frowned. "Then what do you like about her?"

Humoring them, and not having anything else to do, I listened in.

Kyle smirked. "She's beautiful."

My turn to frown.

Aiden beckoned me again. "Come here, cat. We won't hurt you."

Ty ducked low to join Aiden. His gloved fingers hooked on the lattice. "I don't know if this is worth the few bucks."

"Speak for yourself, Ty. My girlfriend says I have to find extra cash for the new game I want. This is easy. Besides, it's fun too."

"Any luck yet?" Kyle asked.

I hadn't moved a muscle.

"Not yet," Aiden said.

"Then you both need to think outside the box," Kyle said. Footsteps climbed the deck above me, and a fist knocked on the door. That couldn't be anything good.

After a beat, hinges squeaked, and a woman's footsteps creaked on the deck. "What's this about?"

"Ma'am, you have a feral cat stuck under your deck. Do you mind if we remove it?"

"Oh!" she said, both surprised and afraid, as if I carried rabies. "Please do. Thank you, young man. Let me know if you need any tools to help."

Excited footsteps rushed back down, and the door above closed. Ty joined Kyle.

Aiden whispered again, "Come here, cat. Quick now, and I'll get you out of here safely. These guys won't be as forgiving."

I could outrun these men easily, but from under the porch, there was only one way to freedom. Kyle and his co-conspirators weren't going to lose interest. I inched closer to Aiden, and when I was within fingertip reach, he rubbed my head. I ducked under his touch and frowned, but I swallowed back my snark.

Aiden's fury unleashed with growls of anger and frustration, and he swiped at me, but I jumped away.

"Did you get it?" Ty asked.

"No. Damn it," Aiden said. "I was close. This close." He held up two fingers, narrowly apart.

So much for being a nice guy. The three of them congregated near the front steps.

"The cat's terrified, and there's only one way out. I have tools in my truck. We're getting that cat with axes if we have to," Kyle said.

With Aiden no longer a crouching guard, I wasn't waiting around to find out just how far they were willing to go. I shimmied through the lattice and bolted off while they were none the wiser.

Chapter 10

So Many Questions

I'd scurried through backyards, under clotheslines, around pools closed for the season, and over chain link fences. Crossing the street during rush hour had been a literal game of chicken. The day had stretched, and now dusk settled on the horizon. I'd had enough of this silly game, but the players hadn't given up yet.

A more pressing concern, the water Mikeal had brought me didn't alleviate the lack of breakfast. I hadn't eaten since yesterday. My stomach grumbled. I wished he'd return—the only friendly face I knew who didn't treat me like an animal or a prize.

The scent of chicken on a grill nearby had me stop and turn. What were the odds I could swipe a piece unscathed?

Following the delicious chicken trail, I zipped along until a flurry of voices and the hissing crack of a can stopped me. I peeked through a hole in the white privacy fence. A woman in an apron held a spatula in front of a smoking grill. Men drank and laughed. Another man, also wearing an apron, stepped out of the house, onto the deck, and handed the woman an empty plate.

There were too many people, and no unattended chicken. I sighed and walked away, head hung low.

"And we meet again." Mikeal's voice. I smiled to myself—not that anyone could tell with a cat's face. How did he sneak up on me so easily? I turned to face him, but my eyes laser-focused on his hand. He pinched a leg of grilled chicken between his fingers. I so desperately wanted it, and even more so to talk to him. My tail flicked with impatience and my stomach grumbled again.

Mikeal leaned back on his haunches and set the chicken down. I looked at him as if asking if this was a trick.

Seeing my hesitation, Mikeal chuckled. "I don't bite, and that's not poison. Eat up. You must be starved after being chased all day."

He didn't have to tell me twice. I tore into the juicy meat while keeping a side eye on the man. His hands were now empty, and he dragged greasy fingers on his pants. No net, no gun, and certainly no leather work gloves. He never made a single move to catch me. If he wasn't playing the game, why was he being so sweet?

Mikeal shifted his weight and settled in the grass, arms casually resting over his knees. "I suppose I could keep you company while you eat."

I sent him a side eye, but I didn't think he could tell.

"It's hard enough to be a vulnerable cat, but when you're so hungry, leaving that meat because you're being chased, is a literal life-and-death choice. So let me make it easier for you."

I relaxed next to him and shook my head, tearing off strips of meat seasoned to perfection.

Mikeal picked at blades of grass. "A long time ago I was offered a job, one considered a great honor in my family, among our clan. I knew the expectation had been on the table since I was young, and although I never encouraged or discouraged my family, I didn't want it—a life of solitude and sadness. It just wasn't for me, but out of respect for my family, and I suppose duty, I accepted it." Mikeal held up the talisman around his neck and studied it. "I told everyone I was honored, and for a while I convinced myself I was, but now it's a weight, dragging me down. You know why?" He smiled at me, sadness tugging at his eyes.

Chapter 11

Not Enough Answers

His voice was like smooth velvet. I could listen to him for hours. It wasn't fair I made fun of the players for talking to me as if a cat understood English, because Mikeal was too. I enjoyed his company. He was kind, thoughtful, and interesting. Although I wanted to know more, I still kept quiet, hoping he'd continue his story.

"Funny you should ask." He chuckled, a soft but deep rumble in his chest. "I told everyone I was honored, because I wanted them to believe they knew what was best for me."

That I understood. Gracie believed the same, and now magic of her design was forcing me to choose someone to marry, and it needn't be said how poor my options were—one of them already had a girlfriend, and another only joined for a cash payment. Why couldn't her magic have foreseen that?

Having someone understand me flooded me with a feeling I'd never had before, and now I wanted to kiss Mikeal. Seeing as I was fur-covered and four-legged, I kept that desire to myself. I leaned down and worked at the next bite of chicken while a blade of grass tickled my eye.

"I opted to keep the truth a secret, rather than live with their disappointment, and now I do my job with a smile on my face—well, not literally. That would be rude and awkward."

My heart broke for him. He was miserable. If I was honest with myself, I didn't want to be Gracie's caretaker. I wanted a life of my own but admitting that left a sour taste in my mouth—bad timing as I chewed delicious chicken. I loved Gracie, and nothing would stop me from my duty to her.

Duty.

I stared. Mikeal and I had a lot in common, even if he was a little odd for having a deep conversation with a cat. Why were we letting our families decide our lives?

"Which leads me to this fascinating game," he continued. "I wonder why Gracie went to such lengths for her daughter. Clearly, she cares very much about Maggie's happiness, even if it's misguided."

Ah, ha! He *was* playing the game—a sneaky, unusually stealthy, and very sexy guy. Well, I kept the key out of arm's reach as I dipped for the last bite.

"But I think Gracie knows her time is running out."

I lifted my head.

"Unlike my family, Gracie knows she placed a burden on her own daughter—and I'm not talking about this game. The guilt of watching Maggie spend her life portioning medication, fluffing pillows, and vacuuming at just the right speed at the right time and going over the same spot the right number of times when she should have her own career, her own family, her own hobbies is an incredible burden. The overbearing guilt pushed her to do this."

I swallowed a thick lump. His detail was almost too good. Was he a caretaker too?

"I know the type." He smiled reassuringly. "But I have to admit this creative game she concocted is a first for me."

Me, too.

He leaned in close. "I think it sucks."

I held back a snort of laughter, but it was damned hard. I hadn't laughed in a long time. I almost forgot how much fun it was—or would've been had I let myself enjoy it. I caught my eyes roaming the stranger's body. Well-kept and nice-shaped, he had curves in the right places—pecs and biceps—ridges where they belonged, and abs showing through his thin T-shirt. What was his burdensome job? Those piercing blue eyes still sparkled in the fading light, and my heart skipped a beat.

"She means well. The fastest way to get a bunch of men interested in her daughter was to make a game of it. She's clever." Mikeal smiled at me and waited.

Since he wasn't trying to net, kick, or shoot me, I found his long chatter endearing, if not a little strange. But honestly, I really liked the company. I would've preferred to be in my human form so I could participate but having someone by my side was better than being alone.

An ambulance's sirens wailed in the distance, growing by the moment. Mikeal craned his neck in that direction with sadness on his features. He sighed and stood up, brushing grass off his pants. "I was too late, and now I must go."

I turned to see the approaching lights, and when I turned back, he was gone.

How did he do that?

Chapter 12

Caught

I TROTTED ALONG WITH the sirens, increasing my speed as the ambulance turned the corner to our block. My heart punched into my throat, and I bolted through the remaining backyards and stopped at our house. The front door was open, and I darted inside. Sprawled on the floor, with the landline handset a few inches from her hand, Gracie's gasps were raspy like she struggled to drag in breaths. Tears filled my eyes.

"Mom!" I whispered before the medics could hear.

Her eyes fluttered open and closed. "No...regrets." Her lips lifted into a small smile and then it faded away.

The men rushed to her side, and I hung back, acting like a normal cat as much as I could while wanting to help—to explain her issues, to tell them about her bum leg, but I couldn't. Even to help save Gracie's life, I couldn't expose our world.

The medics spoke loudly and clearly to her, not knowing if Gracie was hard of hearing. She certainly wasn't, but she didn't respond. They worked on her with tubes and wires and machines that beeped and talked. I understood she had no pulse, but they were fighting to bring her back.

Whatever happened to her in my absence would never have happened. I could've called emergency services sooner. I could've brought her to the emergency room earlier. Why did she put this stupid spell on me? I swiped my eyes with a paw.

The medics lifted her onto the stretcher and rolled her out the door into the dark void of night. Her face was calm, peaceful, asleep. I needed answers. I needed to know what happened. The only way I was going to find out anything was if someone was willing to talk to me—without a gun or a net or gloved hands reserved for feral beasts.

I needed Mikeal.

I'd never seen him around a vehicle. He'd always appeared and disappeared silently. So, rushing with newfound energy, I darted all over the neighborhood, searching for him with my heightened feline senses, trying to pick up his scent or a flicker of movement. I wanted to call for him, but I couldn't risk such blatant exposure. I wished I had his phone number, but even if I did, I couldn't dial with a fluffy paw.

Panting like a sprinter in the desert without water, tears formed in my eyes. I stopped to take a breath. How could Gracie force me to be helpless when she was so vulnerable? And now when she needed me at her hospital bedside, I couldn't be there. She was old, but she wasn't crazy. Her mind was intact, so why the terrible judgment?

Hands pressed the ground on either side of me, and a net I couldn't see squeezed my body down to the grass. "Gotcha."

My blood chilled to my bones at Kyle's voice. At least he learned to warn me *after* he netted me, but I wasn't in the mood to entertain him, and his timing was incredibly in poor taste. If I gave Kyle the key, I could break this curse on me and rush to Gracie's side. It was an easy and efficient solution, but could I live with the consequences? Would Gracie want me to be miserable with Kyle for the rest of my life? I loved Gracie more than anything, but I hesitated.

Kyle lifted me off the ground, fist squeezing the loose net to keep me inside it. In the dark with streetlights casting a yellow glow, menacing shadows danced on his face. His blond hair was disheveled, and he smelled like old taco wrappers. But it was the snarl on his lips, a dark and dirty curl of victory that drained the blood from me.

Chapter 13

Game Over

IT WASN'T THE TERRIFYING look on Kyle's face that had me making up my mind, but it was a big factor. He meant to wish me bodily harm, and what kind of decent man could hurt an animal? One I never wanted to be near, and one I could never marry no matter how much I wanted to see Gracie. She would understand. I curled around the key, leaving him no choice but to open the net and reach inside...and he'd regret it.

"We still get a cut for helping, right?" Aiden asked, but Kyle ignored him.

"Hey, you got her," Ty said, surprised.

"Sure did. Told you so." Kyle lifted me into the air like a child showing off a goldfish won at the fair. He brought me into the cone of light from the streetlight. "Stupid cat."

Open the net and see who's stupid.

Kyle reached in, painfully squeezing various furred body parts, seeking the key around my throat. "And now I don't have to wait for the old bat to kick off. Seems like someone was looking out for me. I don't mind consoling the heartbroken beauty for a few days."

Fighting away tears at his callous comment, I had to do whatever necessary to stop this jerk from getting the key. I leaped at his face and extended my claws, but my back feet were caught in the net. In a flash, I hooked into his skin—forehead and cheek—with my tiny claws, holding on deeply.

Kyle yelled in pain and fury. With both hands, he pulled on me while demanding help. I was too busy to see if either of them attempted to assist. The harder he pulled, the nastier the damage to his face. Eventually, his human strength tore me away, but regret curled his features into hatred. Kyle threw me to the sidewalk painfully, and the net's metal rim hit my throat. I tried to scramble free, but I was tangled and helpless, like a fish out of water.

Kyle barked orders to his minions. "Goddamned cat! Get my gun out of the cab. I'm going to blast this damned cat to high heaven and take the key."

Ty crossed the street to the lifted pickup, and his cell phone's flashlight flickered around as he rummaged behind the driver's seat.

"That's smart," Aiden said. "Should've done that from the start."

Ty rushed it over and handed it to Kyle. "Is it still here?"

"Poor cat is stunned and trapped," Aiden said, pointing at me, stuck under a yellowy spotlight.

"Then I'll put the beast out of its misery." Kyle pressed the butt of the shotgun to his shoulder, and he aimed for my chest.

I could've tried running and dragging the net, but I wouldn't have gotten far enough to avoid that weapon's blast radius, and Kyle's fury truthfully scared me. By staying put, perhaps he'd see mercy, or the hesitant Ty could convince him otherwise.

The soft clicks of the trigger being squeezed had me trembling. I shook a back paw, trying to free myself from the tangles.

He really meant to kill an innocent animal for a key to my house. I was a stranger to him, and he was unwittingly about to kill the person he wanted to marry. If I told him it was me, breaking the rules of our hidden world, I didn't believe I'd gain mercy. I believed he'd only shoot faster. I squeezed my eyes shut.

I'm sorry, Gracie. I couldn't be there for you. I did my best, but my best wasn't good enough. I hope you'll be okay without me.

"That's enough." Mikeal's voice popped my eyes open. He found me!

Mikeal stood between me and the gun, the barrel pointed right at his stomach.

Chapter 14

The Protector

WHAT WAS MIKEAL THINKING standing between me and a raging lunatic with a loaded shotgun? I had no doubt hunting enthusiast Kyle would shoot Mikeal and claim it was an accident, especially in the dark with a 'beast' on the loose. With his dad a member of the sheriff's department, I was sure the consequences, if any, would be a slap on the wrist. I wanted to cry out not to trust Kyle. I wanted to scream for Mikeal to get out of the way. But not for my convenience, not my comfort, nor to relieve my worries of Gracie, and not to save my life would I break the hidden world rule.

That had worse consequences, but the yearning, so strong and loudly screaming in my head, was hard to temper.

"Where did you come from?" Ty asked, frowning at Mikeal and stepping forward.

"Get out of here. We found it first." Aiden stepped up alongside Ty, but he eyed the shotgun warily and took a step back. Even Kyle's best buddy didn't trust him.

"You got some big brass on you, buddy. I already won, and I'm not giving up my prize. This is loaded, so I suggest you leave now," Kyle said, finger on the trigger. "I won't warn you twice."

Please go, Mikeal, please go and save yourself.

Despite my silent pleading, the sexy stranger didn't budge. Without a word to Kyle, Mikeal calmly swatted the barrel to the side, hard enough that Kyle dropped it, and the gun clattered to the sidewalk.

But rather than retrieve his weapon, opening himself up to a strike, Kyle and his cohorts puffed their feathers and stalked up to Mikeal, reminding me of the scuffle at my front door. Except this time, I believed someone was going to get killed. Over me. A cat with a key. This was ludicrous. Mikeal was gravely outnumbered. I couldn't stand by and watch him get hurt, or worse, on my account.

I hobbled toward the three brutes, painfully dragging the net by my injured back paw, and I leaped up. With the weight dragging me down, I didn't get as high as I wanted to, but a surge of adrenaline pumped through me, and one by one I clawed at their faces and jumped to the next. Last in line was Kyle. Expecting my plan, he caught the net handle, and whipped me to the grass. I landed on my side, wind knocked clean from my lungs. I tugged and pulled to drag in a breath, and as the seconds ticked by, my fear for Mikeal only grew.

Ty folded at his waist, holding his bleeding face, and cursing me. Kyle and Aiden wiped blood away casually like it was ordinary sweat. They looked at their palms.

Mikeal crouched beside me like a shield, and he sent a nasty snarl at the men.

"I'm out of here. Maggie's not worth this," Ty said, standing. "Deal's off." He turned and walked away.

Aiden glanced at me and Mikeal. He assessed Kyle's fury. "I'm not going to jail for some cash. Sorry, dude."

"Wait. You can't quit now. It's right here," Kyle pleaded, but Aiden ran off into the darkness after Ty.

Mikeal freed my paw from the net and sent me a sad smile. He rose to face Kyle. "Your friends are smart. If you want to leave here with all your limbs attached, I suggest you follow their lead, and I better never see you around again."

Kyle snarled at me and Mikeal. "She's not worth this. You can have that nasty cat. I bet she never puts out anyway." Kyle picked up his shotgun and stalked away with short glances over his shoulder.

Alone and safe, Mikeal returned to me. "You saved my life. Thank you."

Likewise, I wanted to say.

"How about we find somewhere warm and safe?" He beckoned me into his arms.

Chapter 15

Cozy

FOR THE FIRST TIME, I didn't mind being picked up, and it had nothing to do with my injured paw. I hobbled toward him, and big, strong arms circled me. I was safe already.

The autumn night left a chill in my feline bones. I was hungry, thirsty, and I just wanted to warm up and see Gracie. Mikeal carried me to an ordinary sedan parked not far away, and he settled me on the passenger seat. So he did use a car like a normal person. It was clean in here, no clutter at all, not even coins or a pen, and I couldn't smell any telltale metal of a gun.

Mikeal dropped into the driver's seat. "I've got a few hours off, so I know where we can go warm up. I bet that chicken didn't last, unless of course, you've been snacking on mice while I was away." He paused for a beat. "I didn't think so."

I licked my lips. After all the running and scratching and my injured paw, I needed a meal to get my strength back up. I stared at him, hoping he understood my affirmation.

Mikeal started the car. He drove us just outside of town and brought us up a long driveway. The house was a single story with beige vinyl siding and a dark brown shingled roof. Smoke puffed out of the brick chimney, and a single light glowed from inside. It looked cozy. He parked in front of the garage and shut off the engine.

"Come with me." He held open the driver's side door, and I jumped across and out and flinched at the strike of pain. I followed him up the porch and inside, limping as I went, but I stopped in my tracks at the crackling fireplace. Warm and inviting, the flickering firelight cast a soft glow around the homey living room. Across from the fire was an overstuffed couch with a blanket draped over it, and next to it was a well-worn recliner. In the middle was a low table with coffee rings on the surface. It was incredibly peaceful.

"Go ahead," he said, encouraging me to approach the fire.

He didn't have to ask twice. I hobbled over to the fire and purred as the warmth embraced me like a fleece blanket. Mikeal rummaged in the kitchen behind me and brought over a bowl of water and a plate of shredded meat.

"I don't normally have cat guests, so pardon the crude offering."

I ate and drank appreciatively, and when I was finished, he cleaned up my dishes for me. Used to being at Gracie's beck and call, having someone serve me felt...weird. Although he seemed extra perceptive to a cat's needs, and I wanted to thank him for his kindness and generosity, I still couldn't risk it.

Mikeal returned from the kitchen and settled on the couch. He patted the seat next to him. He hadn't offered his hand expectantly for the key. He hadn't grabbed me to tear it from my collar. He just sat there now patiently waiting for me to join him. I jumped up. "I'm sure you have so many questions."

More than I could string together coherently.

"You remember that job I told you about, the one I didn't want but I do it with a smile on my face?"

I nodded. Hopefully that wasn't too on the nose. I didn't want to scare him off now.

"It's not explicitly in the job description, but I came to free you."

I'd met a lot of people in my years—townies, tourists, and teens with a lack of judgment, and among those were some nice people, ambivalent people, and bullies. Mikeal was firmly in the nice group; perhaps better to describe him as sweet. The way he'd talked to me so respectfully all this time, and treated me not as a cat, but as a person...

I sucked in a breath. Mikeal had to know what I was. I exhaled and took the biggest risk of my life. "How did you figure it out?" I stiffened at my own words, waiting for his response, hoping against hope he didn't freak out and run away or hit me with a pillow.

Mikeal smiled and chuckled. "You finally trust me. I know more than you realize, Maggie."

Chapter 16

Wrong Answer

He didn't freak out. Relief swept over me at being able to talk to someone at last. "Does that mean you know the objective to this stupid game?"

"You're stuck like that until someone gets the key."

"Close enough." *Until I allow someone to take the key.* "I didn't realize you were playing the game."

"I'm not."

A marriage bound by magic, and I was left with terrible, despicable options, where I'd gladly remain a cat for the rest of my days to avoid. But with Mikeal and his kindness, I thought he'd... I'd hoped he wanted... I calmed my racing thoughts so my voice would remain level. "Don't you want the key?"

Mikeal leaned close. His friendly smile set me at ease, and his piercing blue eyes made my heart skip, but I fought back tears. "If you're offering, I'd be delighted."

I gasped, but now I hesitated. "You understand the consequences to taking it, right? The winner of the key is magically—"

"I understand," Mikeal finished for me.

Nerves tingled all over my body. This was it. Mikeal was going to free me, and I wanted him to free me. I wanted...him. I stepped onto his thigh and tipped my head up, giving him full access to the key attached to my collar.

Mikeal unfastened the key and gripped it in his palm, but nothing happened, no magic swirls, no light show from the spell breaking. I turned around to find somewhere private to attempt to shift.

"Do you want me to take the collar off first? I suppose that would hurt."

I snorted. "I think you're right."

I turned to face him again, and he unfastened the collar. I ducked under the couch blanket and shifted back into my human form without resistance. Like standing up after hours and hours cooped up in a car, I sighed in relaxation. I wrapped the blanket around my torso and stretched with a moan. The torture was over.

Mikeal eyed me, and his cheeks burned bright red. "I'll go find you some clothes." He got up and rushed around the corner, and quickly came back with a stack of clothes. "These are men's, but I'm sure you won't mind, considering the alternative."

I took them. "Thank you. You've done so much for me already."

"Bathroom's that way."

I followed his finger and slipped into the bathroom. Quickly I changed. His clothes were baggy on me, but they smelled like laundry detergent and fresh pine—clean and masculine. I returned barefoot to his side. Even though I'd chosen him, it was still weird to accept a marriage proposal from a stranger, and I still had so many questions. "If you weren't playing the game to free me from the spell, then what were you freeing me from?"

"You're not going to like my answer, but Gracie wanted you to know something."

That was where the familiar saucer came from. He'd borrowed my mother's when he offered me water. Instead of joining the embarrassing scuffle on our porch, he'd hung back to talk to her. "And what's that?"

"'I told you so'. Do you know what that means?"

I scoffed. "She thought I was lonely and miserable. That's why she set me up with this humiliating game, because she wasn't going to be around—" I abruptly stopped as memories of the medics rushing my mother out of the house returned. "Is Gracie okay?" I asked, not knowing how he'd know, but feeling like he would, and even if he didn't, I needed to hear kind words.

Mikeal's lips pressed into a grim line. "I'm afraid not."

I frowned. "What do you mean?"

"My job, as I said, was to free you. Not from this game, but the cards fell that way. I'm sorry to inform you that Gracie has crossed the veil, and that was her parting message for you."

Chapter 17

Refuse to Accept

TEARS SPRUNG TO MY eyes. I shook my head, refusing the finality of the meaning behind those words. "No, that's not right. Mom spoke to me before the paramedics rushed her out. She's fine. I need to go visit her in the hospital."

Mikeal touched my hand. "I'm sorry, Maggie."

Still refusing to believe him, I hugged myself. "How do you know she crossed over? How did she give you that message?"

Mikeal lifted the talisman hanging around his neck. He looked at it like it was...a burden. "I came to collect your mother, but her game had me intrigued. We had a chat, and I granted her a little extra time. With permission, I borrowed a saucer and set out to find you in between souls. Unfortunately, I couldn't gain your trust to restore you to human form on time to say goodbye. For that, I'm sorry. But as I explained, I came to free you from your burden—whether you accept it or not."

What a sucker punch to the gut. I'd never been so insulted. "You manipulated me. You had no intention of catching the key to marry me. All of this was a ruse so I could say goodbye to my mom. Why didn't you just say so?"

"My actions were guided by freeing you from being chased and freeing you from an unwanted marriage."

So he didn't want me in return. I was a favor to Gracie, one he failed to accomplish. "You knew the terms of the game before you accepted that key from me. Even if you had no intention of marrying me, neither of us has a choice now. We're magically bound by the terms of the spell."

"You are free to do as you wish. I'm immune to spells."

The wheels turned. "When you chatted with Gracie, she knew that, didn't she?"

"Yes."

If she allowed this guy to free me from the spell without any intention of marrying me, then why put me through all this in the first place? I was so frustrated. "Why all this humiliation and suffering?"

"I think you know."

The only thing that came to mind was Gracie didn't want me around when she died. Was it shame? Did she not want me calling emergency services on her and prolonging her life? I knew she suffered, but her spirits were high, and until that changed, I thought she wanted to stay by my side. All I could figure was she wanted to go. Gracie wanted to cross the veil and relieve me of my...burden. I blinked away tears. I had to know *how* he did all this. I'd heard of many different supernatural beings, but I was at a loss. "What are you?"

Mikeal hung his head low and lifted the talisman. "This makes me an Angel of Death. I know that's a shock, but I'm not here to take you." Mikeal's lips lifted in an attempt at lightheartedness. It didn't work.

My mouth popped open, but nothing came out.

"Your curse and your burden are now gone. I will leave you to seek out the happiness Gracie wanted for you. And with that, duty calls." Mikeal, the Angel of Death, stood up and stretched. "You're welcome to stay if you want or feel free to take my car."

I stared at him, not wanting him to go, but at the same time I needed to get out of here. "When we first met at the grocer's, Lucy died. That was you, wasn't it?"

"Now you understand." Mikeal quirked up his lips. "If you want to see me again, just kill someone, and I'll be there."

I flinched. "What? You can't be serious."

Mikeal chuckled and dug in a back pocket. "Of course not. Here's my number."

I looked at the card, a standard set of phone digits, and when I looked up, he was gone. I supposed the Angel of Death could fly. At least I wasn't going crazy with his appearing and vanishing. But I was speechless.

Chapter 18

The Digits

A short while later, I'd settled most of Gracie's estate. Closing her few accounts and selling off her clothes and medical equipment kept my hands and my mind busy. It even distracted me from my angry ankle. The brutal task, where I'd spent every few minutes breaking into sobs, was finished.

I sat on the couch, sipping from my steaming coffee mug, ankle raised with an ice pack. It was still swollen and uncomfortable. I considered keeping Gracie's walker, but I could make do without. A small part of me wanted the pain, a punishment for not saving my mom, but I hated the constant reminder of Kyle's menacing face. Luckily, Mikeal's warning was heeded, and Kyle had never dropped by.

The television didn't interest me, and I couldn't keep my mind focused on books. I sighed and rotated the melting ice pack. The house was eerily quiet, empty, lacking a soul. I'd dedicated the last few years of my life to Gracie, and now she was gone. As Mikeal said, I was free, but I missed her so much my chest ached.

I didn't feel free.

What was I supposed to do now? There were a dozen hobbies that caught my attention at one point or another over the years. I could attempt to learn them now, but nothing tapped that dopamine trigger in my brain, and I wasn't interested in spending more time alone.

I could get a cat—nah. Not only was I not going to be a crazy cat lady but staring at my alter ego all day and wondering what ticked inside its silent head would drive me crazy, looping me exactly into what I didn't want.

I could call one of my not-as-bad blind dates and see if he'd like a second chance or at least some company. But after that embarrassing public game, instead of being ignored while choosing dinner options, I caught grimaces from various elderly locals—likely family of the men who'd participated in the game. I wasn't sure I wanted to step foot in the dating pool again with an even worse reputation.

I sipped from my mug again and stared at the card resting on my coffee table next to my ankle. Mikeal freed me from a humiliating curse without trying to use me or hurt me. He'd treated me like a human the whole time—because he knew. Would those monsters—Kyle, Aiden, and Ty—have treated me well if they knew I was a human?

Not likely. They still would've run for their guns, their nets, and their leather gloves, because it wasn't me they wanted. They relished the game, the hunt, and I was an elusive door prize.

The truth hit me all at once: I was miserable and alone. Gracie's words, *I told you so*, rang in my ears. She was right, but she'd never get the chance to gloat in my face. Honestly, I'd take her gloating, complaining, wild stories, and unwanted encouragement over nothing any day. I wished I didn't fight my mother's endless schemes to prevent exactly where I was today, because then I wouldn't be, and she and I could've had more quality time together. Hindsight was a tormenting bitch.

Mikeal went above and beyond by granting Gracie more time than she was owed, and he tried to encourage me to trust him, so I'd have more time with her. For a burdensome job he didn't like, he was thoughtful and kind. I loved my mother with every fiber of my soul, but Mikeal was right too. I had been exhausted—physically and mentally—and held back from experiencing life.

After quiet introspection that only death—and the questions of mortality and meaning of life—could bring, now I could do what I always wanted to do. I now knew what that was—to find someone who respected me and wanted to spend time with me. Someone present and available and willing to dote on me once in a while.

Was it selfish?

Yes.

Did I feel guilty about it?

Yes.

But maybe if I helped Mikeal the way he helped me, then the guilt would ease. I pictured Mikeal, the Angel of Death, and wondered what his wings looked like—jet black like a raven's? Only one way to find out.

I picked up the card and dialed the digits. My call went straight to voicemail, catching me off guard. I never expected that, so I left him a message, knowing my nerves trembled my voice. "Mikeal, hi. It's me, Maggie. I was just calling to see if you, I don't know, want to hang out or something? I'd like to talk to you, if you're ever available or interested or something." I pulled the phone away from my ear to hang up, but I didn't give him my number. I rattled off my own cell number and hung up awkwardly.

Now what?

I finished my coffee and cleaned the house again, because I had nothing else to do, and I winced through my ankle's protests. When Mikeal magically appeared again—*if* he appeared—I wanted the house to look and smell nice. Maybe I should redecorate, make the place look like mine now. Then I wouldn't feel waves of despair whenever some inanimate object triggered my memories.

Now I had a plan, something for me, something to look forward to.

Chapter 19

Advice

On a step stool above the kitchen sink, I pounded the stubborn nail over and over. It must've been aimed at a loose lathe strip because the damned thing was *bouncing* as I hit it. Grumbling under my breath, I slammed the nail again, but it bent, half-cocked. I shouted in frustration and clawed the stupid nail out with the back of my hammer. Redecorating turned out to be more frustrating than fun without an extra hand to help, and I looked at my bags full of new décor with overwhelmed eyes.

I kept expecting to hear Gracie's commentary behind me—especially about the bonus holes in the walls—but there was nothing but silence. Emptiness. My attempts to spruce up the place for my mental health seemed fruitless.

Mikeal hadn't called me back. I kept replaying my embarrassing voicemail, wondering if I'd given him the wrong digits, but I was sure I said them right, plus he could hit the call back button. Maybe beyond the veil didn't get cell reception or maybe he was too busy collecting souls to spend a few minutes with me. They were legit excuses, but that wasn't what I wanted in a partner. Good thing I was only offering to help him with his problem: Stand up for himself, so he could figure out what he wanted too. It only seemed fair after how much he did for me.

I tossed the bent nail into the kitchen sink and grabbed a fresh one from the box. I aimed it a little below the old hole and smacked the hammer against it. So far, so good. I finished hammering that nail in and hung up my rustic wood decoration, a sign that read, 'No regrets.'

I climbed down the step stool and smiled at it. My smile faltered at all the damage to the plaster, but hey, I got the job done. Next on my list was a motivational quote over the headboard in my bedroom.

A knock on my door turned my head. Crossing the living room, I checked the peephole. Mikeal stood on my doorstep in his classic dark jeans and a tight T-shirt, but this time, there was no over shirt covering him up, the talisman was gone, and I could see curves that made me sigh. I swallowed back my silly smile and opened the door.

While concentrating on not drooling, I dropped the hammer, and it hit the floor with a startling thud. My face heated, and as I bent to retrieve it, Mikeal reached down to help.

"Slippery little suckers, aren't they?" he asked, handing me the hammer.

Thick biceps pressed against the thin fabric, and I caught a peek in the dipped V of his shirt—rounded pecs just begging to be squeezed and teased. "I can handle the hammer. It's getting nailed that's harder. The sign. Getting the sign nailed—hung." I stumbled over my words, and a rush of heat tore up my chest, neck, and face.

Mikeal grinned with amusement. There was something different about his demeanor, how he held himself. He seemed...less troubled, more relaxed.

"You know what I mean," I finished, lamely.

Mikeal stood there, and like an idiot, I finally registered what he was here for. “Oh, let me get your keys. I had your clothes washed too.” I hobbled back toward my kitchen and collected the neatly folded pile. When I turned around, Mikeal had followed me inside.

“How’s your ankle?”

“Still hurts, but I manage.” I handed him the stack, but he set it right back where I had it.

“I can fix it, if you’ll let me.”

He offered to put his hands on me. *Yes, please*. But what I was thinking wasn’t what he had in mind. “Um, I have a wrap bandage around here somewhere. I wasn’t using it because the ice works fine whenever it acts up.”

“That won’t be necessary.” Mikeal scooped me up into his arms, and in surprise, I gripped his firm shoulders. Yet another flash of heat rushed through me. Mikeal carried me to the couch and set me down gently. Tingling with excitement and anticipation, I waited for him to do whatever he wanted to my body.

Mikeal crouched by my feet and tugged up the tight jeans over my right ankle, and imagining his hands exploring farther, I bit back a grin. But Mikeal was a good doctor, focused on the injury. He curved his hands on either side of my ankle, touching gently, and after a beat, the throbbing ache and sharp pains eased until they were gone. Just like that, Mikeal replaced my jeans. "Better?"

I rolled my ankle around, surprised. "Yeah, it is. Thank you."

Mikeal beamed with pride, and he sat next to me. "So, I got your message. You wanted to talk?"

Thrilled to be relieved of the constant reminder of Kyle, nerves had me rise to my feet. "I do. Would you like a drink?"

Mikeal took a deep and obvious whiff of the air. "Coffee sounds great." Mikeal rubbed his hands on his thighs.

I peeled my eyes away from wanting to do just that, and I carried my hammer to the kitchen counter. Moving the step stool out of the way made more noise than I'd expected.

Curiosity brought Mikeal over. He leaned against the counter. "I like your sign. I think you did a good job, commanding that hammer," he said, pointing up at my dents, dings, and extra holes in the plaster.

"It's the last thing my mom said to me, and I intend to live by it."

"That sounds like an excellent plan."

With a stupid smile on my face, I poured him a mug full and got myself a refill. I handed him one, and with a steamy gaze beckoning him to follow, I returned to the couch. He got the message. Legs nearly touching, Mikeal sipped the hot brew and waited expectantly.

I stared into his piercing blue eyes and concentrated on my practiced speech, so I didn't sound like a dope this time. "You helped me a lot, Mikeal, changed my life, even, and I thought—I hoped—I could help you, for what little it might be worth."

Amused, Mikeal sipped. "How so?"

I didn't know how he was going to take my advice, so I just spit it out. "Quit."

"Quit?" He lifted his brows at me.

"Put in your notice and quit your job. I can see it makes you miserable, and that's no way to live your life." It was something I'd guessed from his monologues while I was a cat, but seeing the change in him today, I knew I was onto something. Mikeal stared at me, processing, and I backpedaled. "Unless you don't want to, then don't mind me."

Chapter 20

Hope Blooms

I HOPED I DIDN'T insult him. I truly meant well. I wanted him to be happy, and clearly his burdensome job was dragging him down—something I now understood intimately, except he could escape his while I had to wait out mine. Rest in peace, Gracie.

Mikeal set the mug on the table. "No, no, it's good advice. Just a little late."

"What do you mean?"

"When I was adamant you should live your own life, passionate even, about you being able to take command of your life and live it the way you wanted to, I truly believed it. After pondering the advice, I decided I should take it myself. Turn over a new leaf. So I quit." He pressed a palm against his chest, right where the talisman had been. "Because of you, I'm no longer an Angel of Death. I'm a new man."

"Congratulations." I was proud of him, but still curious. This new man could heal injuries, but since he wasn't a vampire, my encyclopedia of supernaturals didn't cover him. "So what does that make you now? A fallen angel?" I hoped I didn't inadvertently ruin his life.

"Well," Mikeal glanced at the ceiling in thought. "I suppose I'm just an ordinary, boring elf now."

I must've heard wrong. I set my mug on the coffee table next to his. "Elf?"

"Angel of Death was a job title given to me. I was one of many, and it sounds more ominous than it is. But me, the real Mikeal, I'm an elf—ears, wings, immortality—the whole works. Healing is one of my specialties."

I cackled. "Ha! I knew you could fly. There was no other way for you to disappear on me so fast. Can I see them?"

Mikeal stood and craned his neck around as if judging his space. "Ready?"

I nodded enthusiastically.

With a shift of his shoulders, broad wings—not jet black at all, but white with gold flecks—spanned most of my living room. They were stunningly gorgeous. "I can see why you're mistaken for an angel."

“Most people can't see them unless I want them to, and I become invisible when the wings lift me up. It’s a self-defense thing. You know, keeping the hidden world hidden.”

I smiled. “I do. Immortal, huh? So would Kyle’s shotgun have hurt you?”

“Stung, but as long as I could dig out the poisonous metal shell casing, it’s not fatal.”

I was relieved to hear it. “Then how old are you? Is it rude to ask? I’ve never met an elf before.”

“How old do I look?”

The thick dark hair with flecks of gray and the scxy lines around his eyes screamed healthy and stable, but still full of stamina. “Firmly distinguished.”

“I’ll take it.” He dug in his back pocket and returned to the couch next to me. “Listen, you should have this.” He offered me my front door key. “It’s yours. You should keep your door locked, for safety, especially with those wild guys out there. You never know what mischief might wander through your door."

I left his palm hanging. "I have one last question for you. Why me? Why did you help me?"

Mikeal cleared his throat. "Well, I should think it was obvious." I didn't respond, so he continued, "I was summoned to take Gracie across the veil, and the story of her game intrigued me, true, but that wasn't enough for me to grant her the extra time. It was you. When I found out you, Maggie, were subject to the game, the beautiful woman at the grocery store who selflessly dedicated her life to others, I wanted to help. I wanted to see you again."

Chapter 21

No Regrets

No one before had ever spoken to me like Mikael just did. My chest swelled with his sweet words. He was everything I'd hoped for and more than I wished for. So now it was my turn to give him my decision, to tell him just what I wanted. I reached for the key, but instead of taking it from his palm, I wrapped his fingers over it. "Keep it."

Mikeal's hot gaze swept over me, leaving my body flashing with heat and desire. "What exactly does this mean?"

I'd only just met him, so getting married was nuts, but thankfully the magic spell couldn't force Mikeal to do anything. Since he freed me to choose who I wanted, I chose Mikeal and only Mikeal. "It means I want to see you again. I've been through a lot lately, so I prefer to take things slow—one step at a time—and if things lead that way, I'm not opposed."

Mikeal stood and pocketed the key. He held out a hand to assist me standing up. Inches from his handsome face, his hand released mine and strong arms wrapped around me. Broad hands pulled me close. "How slow?"

His eyes watched my lips, and my breath caught. "Not too slow." I leaned forward and kissed him.

After his initial surprise, Mikeal kissed me back. His arms shifted to press me against his firm chest, and I sensed his desire against my hip. Heat bloomed in my body from my chest down low, and tingles trailed along with it. I pulled back, panting. "Bedroom's this way."

"Only if you allow me to make dinner afterward."

"Oh, I don't know. That's some serious commitment." I smiled. "Dinner sounds yummy. What did you have in mind?"

"I was thinking shrimp fettuccine Alfredo. You seemed enthusiastic when I was reading the label." Mikeal grinned, those lovely lines crinkling around his blue eyes, and he lifted me into his arms.

“It’s like you can read my mind.”

“I’ve learned to be observant, but I should warn you, I might look like an angel, but there's nothing angelic about me."

I smiled against his lips. "Good. I didn't want to be judged anyway."

Mikeal groaned. "Am I going to find a bunch of hammer holes in the bedroom? I'm all for kink, but I do have my limits to how much pain I like.”

“I don’t have a pain-inflicting kink, and I think you’ll be too busy to notice my walls, but if you're offering an extra hand—”

"I'd be delighted to assist with whatever hammering you have in mind," Mikeal finished for me.

"Perfect."

Mikeal found my lips again, and we stumbled and shuffled into the bedroom, racing to remove each other’s clothing and take in the beautiful sights before us. As I’d pictured, he was lean and cut. Thick muscle covered his broad frame—not too much that I questioned his hours at the gym, but enough to be appreciated. His silky boxers dropped to the floor, and I marveled at what greeted me.

Wracked with nerves, heart thundering in my chest, I jumped his bones, knocking him to my mattress. I took his lips and trailed butterfly kisses down his neck, while a happy length bobbed for attention.

"I thought you wanted to take it slow," he said, panting.

"What can I say? You're simply irresistible."

Mikeal groaned and gripped me tight. He spun us over with me bouncing onto the mattress under him. "And so are you." Hungry lips explored every inch of my body while I tilted my head back, enjoying every sensitive touch and tingle. And when his length filled me up, I cried out in sweet need.

There was definitely plenty of hammering.

I was happy, Gracie. *Don't worry about me. I have no regrets.*

Dear Reader,

Want to join the reader's club and be the first to know about new releases, sneak peeks, and other fun stuff? Join on my website: StephanieFlynn.net.

As an indie author, I'm thrilled you shared your time with me, exploring the crazy worlds residing in my head and keeping me up at night. Your reviews are very important to me, so if you enjoyed this book, please consider leaving some stars for Mikeal and Maggie's story, **Love Claws**.

Discover more titles at StephanieFlynn.net/books.

If you found any typos or errors, please submit them to: stephanie@stephanieflynn.net.

Thank you for your support!

ALSO BY STEPHANIE FLYNN

Immortal Protector series

0.5 Vampire's Distraction

1 Vampire's Deception

2 Vampire's Secret

3 Vampire's Promise

Matchmaker in Time series

0.5 Minutes to Live

1 Seconds to Act

2 Hours to Arrive

3 Days to Hide

4 Years to Savor

Pirates in Time series

1 Pirate's Prize

2 Pirate’s Treasure

3 Pirate’s Plunder

Standalones

One Crazy Time

Fateful Time

Love Claws

ABOUT STEPHANIE FLYNN

Stephanie Flynn writes action-packed paranormal romance filled with adventure, suspense, and danger. She lives in Michigan, USA, with her husband and kids, and she spends her writing time surrounded by a herd of normal cats who bat everything off her desk, including her coffee. Check out her website for more books: StephanieFlynn.net

CPSIA information can be obtained
at www.ICGtesting.com
Printed in the USA
LVHW100025150123
737059LV00004B/245

9 781952 372711